No New Baby

*For siblings who have a
brother or sister die before birth*

By Marilyn Gryte

Illustration and design
by Kristi McClendon

Copyright©1988
Revised 1999
All Rights Reserved
Centering Corporation

ISBN #1-56123-041-3
San: 298-1815

Centering Corporation
1531 North Saddle Creek Road, Omaha, NE 68104
Phone: 402-553-1200   Fax: 402-533-0507
Email: J1200@aol.com

Dear Parents and Grandparents,

If you are reading this little book to a child it's likely because you have needed to say goodbye to a baby you wanted in your family. You deserve comfort and support.

Parents and other caring adults often wrestle with what to tell children about a miscarriage, stillbirth or newborn death. "Protecting" children from loss and sadness often isolates them and increase their apprehension. They sense something is wrong. Help them put words to it. The very act of sitting and reading to them is reassuring and comforting.

We offer you some guidelines:

◉ Be open with children about sadness and loss. They learn how to grieve in healthy ways by being with adults who allow honest feelings.

◉ Answer questions simply and briefly. It's okay to not know why this has happened.

◉ Use honest words like "died" rather than "gone". It will be less confusing to children.

◉ Give an explanation children can grow up into - rather than giving a different version at each developmental stage.

◉ Children easily presume harm is their fault. Reassure them they are not to blame. - even if they haven't put their fear into words.

◉ Children sense distress in the family. Offer extra cuddling and closeness. This can be comforting to parents as well.

◉ Provide a familiar routine to children even in the midst of sadness.

◉ Whenever appropriate include children in goodbye rituals. They can offer a drawing or small toy as a way of participating.

◉ Remember the support they receive at this time will make later losses in their life more manageable.

The loss of a baby during pregnancy or near the time of birth is a lonely loss easily minimized by society. Remember you have the right to be sad for as long as you are sad. You have a right to honor the due date of your baby. Not everyone will understand this - find those who do and receive comfort from them.

We're sorry this little book is needed. We hope it is helpful to you and the children you love.

Marilyn

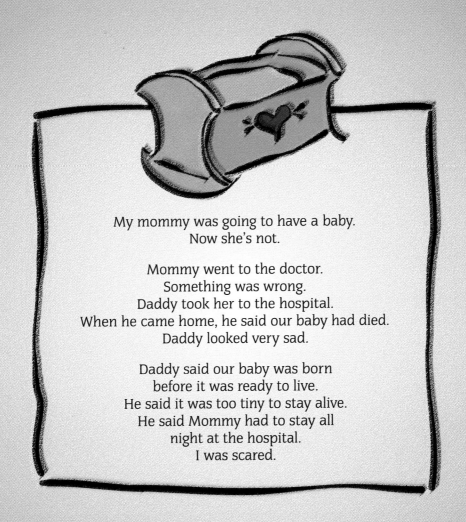

My mommy was going to have a baby.
Now she's not.

Mommy went to the doctor.
Something was wrong.
Daddy took her to the hospital.
When he came home, he said our baby had died.
Daddy looked very sad.

Daddy said our baby was born
before it was ready to live.
He said it was too tiny to stay alive.
He said Mommy had to stay all
night at the hospital.
I was scared.

Daddy read to me and tucked
me into bed.
I hugged Penguin tight and
looked at my night light.
"I wish Mommy was here," I said.
"I wish everything was OK."
"Me, too," Daddy said.
Then he kissed my forehead.

When Mommy came home,
she hugged me and cried.
The baby wasn't in her tummy anymore.
Daddy looked like he had been crying, too.
I was sad.

When the baby was inside Mommy,
I patted her tummy. I could feel the baby kick.
One time I patted really hard.
"Ouch! Be careful!" Mommy said, then she
hugged me and laughed.

I had helped to get Baby's room ready, too.
"Come on, Big Sister!" Daddy had yelled.
"Let's get the baby crib."
He carried me piggy-back all the way to the garage.
Together we carried the crib inside and washed it.
Mommy got out my Winnie-the-Pooh sheets
and my teddy bear blanket.
"How come Baby gets my playroom
for a bedroom?" I had asked.
I liked it better just the way it was.

I didn't like everybody changing things
around just because of a baby.
Sometimes I didn't want a new baby at all!

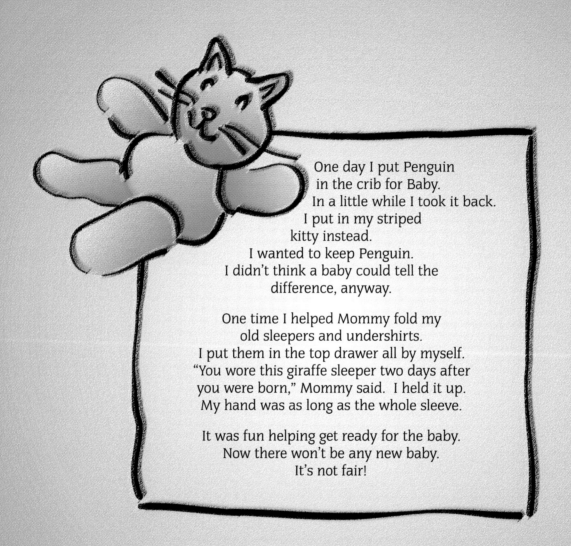

One day I put Penguin
in the crib for Baby.
In a little while I took it back.
I put in my striped
kitty instead.
I wanted to keep Penguin.
I didn't think a baby could tell the
difference, anyway.

One time I helped Mommy fold my
old sleepers and undershirts.
I put them in the top drawer all by myself.
"You wore this giraffe sleeper two days after
you were born," Mommy said. I held it up.
My hand was as long as the whole sleeve.

It was fun helping get ready for the baby.
Now there won't be any new baby.
It's not fair!

It's like saying there's going
to be a birthday party
with balloons and
ice cream and then
there isn't one after all.

It's like waiting for your friend to
come and play and she doesn't show up.

Grandma came over this morning.
"Let's go to the park and swing," she said.
I love going to the park with Grandma.
She tells me stories.
She knows things, like why there's water
in clouds and how butterflies fly.

7

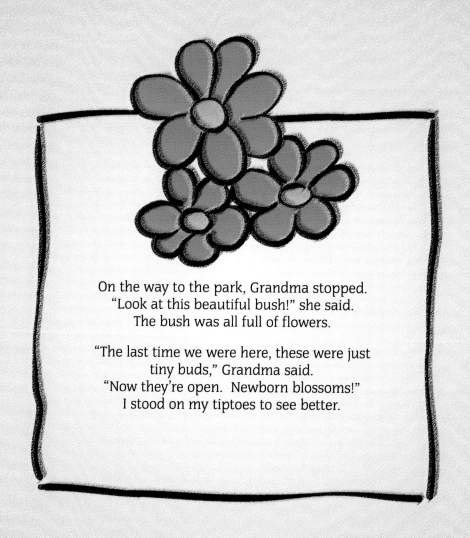

On the way to the park, Grandma stopped.
"Look at this beautiful bush!" she said.
The bush was all full of flowers.

"The last time we were here, these were just
tiny buds," Grandma said.
"Now they're open. Newborn blossoms!"
I stood on my tiptoes to see better.

"Grandma, why did our baby die?" I asked.
"Why was Baby born too soon?
Did I do it when I patted too hard?
Sometimes I didn't want a new baby."

Grandma gave me a big, soft hug.
"No," she said. "The baby didn't die
because you patted hard.
Nothing you said or did or thought
could ever make Baby die.

It's nobody's fault. It just happened.
I don't know why."

It wasn't like Grandma
not to know.

Grandma took hold of my hand.
She leaned over and
picked something up
off the ground.
"See this little bud?" she asked.
"It was supposed to keep growing
and turn into a flower.
But it didn't, and no one knows why.
Most little buds become flowers, but some don't.
This one died.
It will never be a flower now.

I held the bud in my hand.
"Just like our baby," I told Grandma.
I felt sad inside.

Grandma swung with me for a long time.

I pumped so high I could see almost to China
and clear past Jason's house.
Before we went home Grandma hugged me again.
"We're sad because our baby died," she said.
"And it's OK to be sad.
We're still a family and we love each other."

When we got home, I walked over to Jason's.
He's learning to ride a two-wheeler
and he likes me to watch.
I'm learning to skate, and sometimes
I like him to watch.

Jason wants to own a
candy store when he grows up.
I want to grow up and be a doctor.

But right now, I just want to be a big sister.
Maybe someday.

I hope so.